Michael Kleeberg
The Communist of Montmartre

Translated by David Dollenmayer

ERIS
gems

IN APRIL 1935, THE PARIS CENTRAL of the Communist Party found itself in an acutely embarrassing dilemma. Moscow had asked them to bring one representative from each ethnic group oppressed by French imperialism to the Festival of Peace scheduled for that coming summer.

But although when they went through the membership rolls it was no trouble at all to find a trustworthy Algerian and an active Vietnamese, likewise Polynesians and Caribbean mulattoes who enthusiastically embraced the directive to accompany the French delegation, nevertheless, search the ranks of the party as they might, no representative of the exploited of black Africa was to be found.

Gaspard Morand, whom the Central Committee had assigned to organize the French delegation, thought he had saved the day when, in a misplaced card file, he finally sniffed out the trail of a certain Idriss Wakabe. But then he learned from the treasurer that the man in question had been expelled from the party more than a year ago for repeated failure to pay his dues. Not yet fully realizing the difficulties awaiting him, the outraged Morand rejected out of hand the suggestion that the problem could be solved by simply readmitting Wakabe, despite his lack of solidarity.

"This trip is an honor," he declared categorically. "There can be no question of allowing a profiteer to profit from it!"

But then whom could they send?

The party activists were dispatched to scare up a suitable black from their district or circle of acquaintances, on the condition that he really come from Africa and be willing to become a member of the party. They all returned empty-handed.

They either found no one at all, or they found someone who fit the description and would have taken the trip to the Soviet Union, just not at what was, in fact, the very high price of losing his job by missing work for two weeks.

Finally, as the deadline for visa applications drew nearer and nearer, Gaspard Morand found himself compelled to take out a classified ad. Just to be on the safe side, he published it not just in the party paper, but also in the *Figaro*. It read as follows: "Humanistic organization seeks black African for two-week educational trip to friendly nation. Entertainment included. Respond to Box 457."

Morand was quite proud of the cryptic wording necessitated by the circumstances, but three days after the ad had appeared this feeling gave way to a growing panic when only a single, solitary letter awaited him in the box at the *Figaro*. He skimmed the three or four barely legible and error-filled lines, which to his astonishment were written on the finest-laid paper and stated simply that the undersigned, one L.L., met the conditions, loved to travel, and had the time.

Morand, who didn't have much choice left, wrote back immediately, inviting the putative African to party headquarters on the day after next.

On Wednesday morning, sitting at his shabby desk among mountains of paper, he could hear a murmuring from the hall, but before he had time to wonder what it was about, the door flew open and on the threshold stood Marie, the secretary of the section, her hand over her mouth and her eyes wide. Then she announced, "Monsieur Lammermoor."

"Di Lammermoor, please! Luciano di Lammermoor! Actor and vaudeville artiste, at your service!"

Enveloped in a cloud of perfume (jasmine or lavender, was Morand's involuntarily guess; he was unable to afford such luxuries for his wife), a Negro sashayed into the smoky office with a broad grin, removed his boater, and bowed, flourishing the straw hat before him like a musketeer. He wore a yellow-checked, custom-made suit with flashy suspenders, a black shirt, a red tie, and socks to match—that is, they matched the tie.

Morand, his mouth agape, had two thoughts simultaneously. He was unable to get his brain to analyze the situation more thoroughly or his mouth to utter a greeting or any other response. He thought, "Thank God he *is* black," then, "I'll be damned, a queen."

Once he had recovered from the sight of the man before him and offered him a chair, Morand lit a cigarette and, after brief consideration, decided to come out with the truth without beating around the bush.

"We're looking for an African Negro to accompany a delegation to the Soviet Union as a party member," he said, and gazed at the black man from beneath knitted brows.

"Of course," di Lammermoor answered with a smile, "at your service," and lit up a cigarette as well, having first inserted it into an ivory holder.

"We are the French Communist Party," said Gaspard Morand, more in inquiry than as a test.

The black man leaned back, took a drag, and held the cigarette out in front of him, his fingers extended. As if stupefied, Morand stared at the circle of his mouth, from which issued little smoke rings.

"I offer my talents to anyone who knows how to appreciate them." Here he leaned forward a little and rubbed his thumb and index finger together. "Moreover," he added in between smoke rings, "I've never gone on tour in that part of the world."

Morand closed his eyes for a moment.

"You're familiar with the party?" he then asked.

The black man gave a roguish smile and waved his hand before his face in a vague gesture, as if he had been asked about a play by an unknown author but with actors he had heard about somewhere.

"But you're not a member of some other party?" Morand inquired warily.

Lammermoor burst out laughing. Then he said seriously, "I'm an *artist*."

"Eh, an artist...?"

"Yes, until recently I had an engagement at the *Chat qui p'che.*"

Morand was familiar with the name. It was a dubious cabaret up on Montmartre where the rich liked to mingle with the *canaille* on Saturday evenings. No honest workingman from the faubourg would ever set foot in it.

"And, eh, what did your work there entail?"

"Ah, wait a second and I'll show you a number," cried Lammermoor excitedly. "Of course, it's not the same without my costume, my wig, my *accessoirs*, but it will give you an idea..."

He stood up, placed one foot on the seat of his chair, threw back his head, exhaled smoke through his nostrils, and began to sing. "*Je cherche un millionaire...*"

Morand froze. It was *la Miss*, Mistinguett, unmistakably. There she stood. He forgot he had a Negro in a yellow checked suit in his office, saw only the great Mistinguett.

When di Lammermoor broke off his

imitation and bowed to Gaspard Morand, there was applause and five heads were visible through the partially opened door.

"Bravo!" cried Marie.

"Out! Back to work!" bellowed Morand. "And close the door! We're having an important conference!" He dabbed the sweat from his brow.

"And that's not all," said the Negro. "Naturally I also do Fréhel, Damia..."

"All right, all right," Morand interrupted him, "but we're looking for something along completely different lines. It's a serious matter...the exploitation of the working classes. It's deadly serious, not play-acting..."

"The exploitation of the working classes," said Lammermoor, slowly and reflectively, looking at Morand. He was already seeing him as a director, working up a new part.

"Yes. We're not talking about a theater tour. We're real workers here, really exploited, and our comrades in the Soviet Union have invited us because..."

He glanced at the black and fell silent.

"It's not…a tour?" Lammermoor asked.

Morand bit his lips. He had to choose between his personal principles and the good of the party. Hadn't Lenin said somewhere that the end justifies the means? In two days they had to apply for the visas, and the alternative to this crackpot here was to have to admit to the comrades in Moscow that not a single black in France belonged to the party.

"It's…not a tour in the classic sense. I mean, not in period costumes. It's…more or less…a modern play…" He gasped for breath. "Proletarian theater!" he got out. "An international gathering for cultural exchange!" At least on the last point he wasn't entirely lying.

Lammermoor had recovered his smile.

"Ah, the others are all amateurs!" he cried. "That means I can share my stage experience with them. Very nice. But what will my role be, exactly?"

Morand, whose forehead was pouring sweat, mopped it off with a checkered handkerchief and then reached back with a fierce gesture to dry the back of his neck as well.

"You're to play a black Parisian workingman who has joined the party to improve his working conditions..."

"That's all?" Lammermoor exclaimed in astonishment.

"Don't fool yourself," said Morand grimly. "I can imagine it's pretty difficult to play a life of misery if you've never experienced it."

"I assure you I'm up to the task. It's true, so far I've been featured mainly in the humoristic genre, but a character role is every actor's dream. You know, no one really takes you seriously until you've done one."

There were still two obstacles to be overcome. The first was the visa. The black gave his name as Luciano di Lammermoor and could see no reason whatsoever why the officials should need his real name. In the end, the tormented Morand had to scream at him, "Your name or no tour!" Only then did Lammermoor relent and enter the name Watabe N'Komo on the list.

The second problem was his remuneration for the tour. Naturally, the party had no money in its till for such things, and Lammermoor was unwilling to sell his services for less than they were worth. He declared that in his profession it was impossible to reduce one's price once it had been established. But they finally agreed to meet each other halfway, and the preparations could begin.

Gaspard Morand had to see to all the arrangements for the entire trip, so he delegated a youngster who worked on the assembly line at Citroën—at twenty-one one of the most passionate and hard-working activists—to give Lammermoor a crash course in Communist culture: the most important historical facts, the essential pronouncements of the classic writers, the social situation in France, the party's role in the Comintern, the task of agitation in the light of the revolution, and for good measure the program of the Festival of Peace in Moscow and the part to be played in it by the French delegation. François (that was the name of the young instructor) and the others—all working men from Belleville, Les Halles, or from the assembly line—soon discovered that Lammermoor's education was a reciprocal affair.

For although one could state categorically that the latter had not the faintest notion of Marx, Engels, Lenin, and the Comintern, up to now had not cared a fig about the imperialism of the French colonizers, and to François's horror lacked even a shred of class consciousness, still he knew things—important things, a whole treasure trove of professional tricks and first-hand life experience—which he had no intention of withholding from his new colleagues in view of their upcoming tour.

Social consciousness is the product of the conditions of social life...the forces of production...the circumstances of production... The social character of the production process demands social control of the means of production...the proletarian revolution... Historical necessity does not establish itself automatically but requires the conscious, militant effort of a class-conscious vanguard of the proletariat...the base, the superstructure ("That's what you belong to," said François)...socialist morality (Morand had insisted that François thoroughly inform Lammermoor about the latter)...exploitation, etc., up to and including the black having to memorize the "Internationale."

At first Lammermoor had made little note cards to keep his bearings in the thicket of complicated, similar-sounding terms. As for the application of a phrase in a particular situation, he could rely on his artistic instincts, having quickly grasped that everything was in any event a question of tone of voice, facial expression, pathetic or muted emphasis and thus not as far removed from his métier as he had at first feared.

After a few weeks, several comrades were moved to tears whenever the small, elegant black man stepped forward, removed his boater, clutched it to his chest, and casting an oblique glance up into the blue (or rather up to the low ceiling), launched into "Brothers, Toward Sunlight, Toward Freedom."

François, who had grown fond of him, invited him for a beer one evening after their lesson and asked him about his life.

"How come you joined our ranks? Had enough of living without consciousness? Up to here with being exploited?"

"*Mon petit,*" replied Lammermoor, "let's just say that my last engagement at the *Chat qui p'che* had run out and I was currently, eh, somewhat stranded? A tour like this one was just the ticket. But between you and me, the boss...the director...Morand—he pays pretty damn badly."

"Why are you always talking about a tour and the theater? You must realize who we are by now?"

"The whole world is a theater, *mon petit*, and everyone is playing a role. I don't care what the play is called as long as I'm in the spotlight. And then, watch this. Can you do it better?"

And he stood up, pulled his head down

between his shoulders, and shuffled across the room, dragging an imaginary broom behind him. "Yes, Monsieur, of course Monsieur, at your service, Monsieur..." Then he suddenly straightened up and gave a fiery speech on the necessity of proletarian solidarity, so rapidly that François couldn't follow the details, so red-blooded that he involuntarily squared his shoulders before bursting into laughter and applause, and then suddenly asked in a confidential tone, "And what's it like, then? I mean, the theater and the cabaret? Tell me about it."

"Ah, *mon petit*, it's a different world...a different world." And he dreamily fanned the air before his eyes, as if dispersing wisps of fog that obscured his vision of that wondrous world.

And then he told about how, with a Senegalese sharpshooter for a father, he had grown up alone with his mother in a bordello in the ninth arondissement; how friends (he drew out the word and smiled coquettishly at François) had introduced him to all sorts of things, among others, the world of the music hall; how he had made his first sorties as the evening escort of lonely citizens in Montmartre.

"Do you know Schoudler, the banker?"

"What, that swine of an exploiter?"

"Yes. For a while we were...friends."

"Unbelievable!" François cried. "You know big shots like that in person? And how does he live?"

"Well," answered Lammermoor. "But all alone. And have you ever heard of Baron De Clermont?"

"Who hasn't?"

"Also an acquaintance from those days."

François stared at him, open-mouthed. "And you, you... He scratched his head.

Lammermoor smiled. "They're very generous gentlemen."

François shook his head and murmured, "I'll be damned, with a Negro..." In horror he clapped his hand over his mouth and stammered an apology.

Lammermoor laughed out loud and

showed his dazzling white teeth.

Blushing, François asked, "And the theater, what's it like in the theater?"

"Are you interested?" inquired the other.

"I'm a worker and I'll always be a worker," he said, but his brave tone came out sounding hollow.

"My parody of *la Miss* is famous, you know. Once she was there with her whole entourage and my knees were knocking on stage and I was in mortal fear my wig would slip or my garters snap..."

"Your garters," François echoed. "But you're a man just like me. Aren't you ashamed to wear women's clothes on stage? My God, if one of us did something like that, he'd get a punch in the kisser..."

"Not just on stage, *mon petit*, not just on stage! Why don't you come along tonight? We'll have a look at a show somewhere. Friends of mine are performing."

Lammermoor lived in a boardinghouse at the foot of Montmartre, in a cramped room in which the mess had reached chaotic proportions. Everywhere dresses hung on hangers from the ceiling, feather boas meandered over backs of chairs, high-heeled pumps littered the floor. An unmade canopy bed dominated the middle of the room. François perched on the edge of it, breathing shallowly so as not to fill his lungs with the heavy scent of perfume the closed window prevented from escaping. He opened his top shirt button and kneaded his cap in his hands while Lammermoor changed clothes behind a Japanese screen. He emerged, his muscular black body clad in silk panties and garters, a blonde wig on his head, his lips painted blood red. He pulled on some pumps and then, writhing like an eel, slipped into a tight-fitting green velvet dress.

François was perspiring.

"Would you zip me up?"

François swore under his breath but did what was asked of him.

Then Lammermoor coquettishly took his arm and burst out laughing when the other roughly tried to free himself. The black laid his blonde head on François's shoulder and said, "Shall we go, *mon petit*?"

However much Lammermoor disconcerted his teachers by learning the Communist vocabulary like a stage script without in the least caring what the words really meant and how much earnestness, struggle, and suffering had gone into them, by the same token he was widening their own spectrum, their own world view and knowledge. Namely—at least since the evening with François—he was teaching them what he knew in return: how one behaved at table as a guest of the banker Schoudler in a first-class restaurant, which silverware went to the right of the plate and which to the left, what wine got poured into what glass, how one addressed a woman of the world (if one was confronted with the wife of a fifty-year-old, already past her prime, one bowed to her husband and said, "Ah, Excellency had the splendid idea of bringing his daughter along"), which compliment one made to her and which preferably not—or anyway not in public, which were the good and which the outstanding brands of champagne. And especially for François: how one imitated the walk and gestures of a woman, how one played a role, sang, danced, how one carried oneself on the stage, told off-color jokes so that everyone had to laugh at them, and when one had better be cautious about telling them.

As the day of departure drew near, there was a new source of conflict between Lammermoor and Gaspard Morand, this time about wardrobe.

"But it insults my sense of color!" said the black who, for the final meeting before they left for the station, had appeared in a flamingo-colored suit and spats. He gestured dismissively and with an expression of distaste at the brown and gray caps, jackets, and trousers of the others.

"I don't know why you can't be a Communist and still have good taste, dear fellow. On stage, O.K., I'll wear that stuff, but for the trip...!"

Morand was on the verge of a collapse. Recovering himself, he said pleadingly, "The play isn't just on the stage. It already begins when we board the train. We're not just performing for the Russkies..." And he broke into a sweat imagining the faces of the people on the Central Committee if they were to see his Negro arriving at the station dressed like this.

Finally Lammermoor allowed himself to be persuaded, changed clothes, but arrived at the station with a red camellia in his lapel. Morand's chief nudged him and gestured in Lammermoor's direction. "Nice touch, Morand. We should all do the same. It'll look good when we arrive in Moscow and are wearing something red in honor of the flag. Has he been in the party long then, your little Negro? A good activist?"

Morand mumbled something unintelligible in a choked voice, nodded, and hurried off to join his group.

The program in Moscow went off without a hitch, or almost. The visit to a factory;

the discussion among workers of various nationalities with the help of translators, during which the members of the European delegations got to hear directly from the mouths of their Soviet colleagues how much better the worker had it in the motherland of Socialism; the visit to a *kolkhoz* with the smoke rising from the stacks of the steam threshing machines away to the horizon; an outdoor supper and singing under the stars with the farm workers; the visit to a modern workers' housing project at the edge of Moscow after a bus ride through endless gray suburbs—everything led by Comrade Golubchov accompanied by several other men. He efficiently saw to it that everything went according to schedule, every one of the foreign comrades received extensive information, and none of the lambs went astray.

But two did go astray, and did so on the very eve of the official introduction of the delegations to the Parliament and the Politburo. When Krasskov, one of Golubchov's watchdogs, stepped into the dormitory of the French delegation for taps, and after a superficial inspection asked Morand if everyone was present and accounted for, the latter feared his red face would betray him as he replied, "All present and accounted for! Good night, Comrade! Tomorrow will be a great day!"

It was Lammermoor and François who were missing, of course, and Morand was sweating blood and water and wishing them both before a drumhead court-martial when, about 3:00 a.m., there came a knock at the window and the two night owls scrambled in.

Lammermoor gave him a broad grin. "We were taking a look at Moscow nightlife."

"There is no ènightlife' in Moscow!" bellowed Morand. He winced at his own voice and continued in a furious whisper, "This is a workers' and peasants' state here! It's got nothing to do with the capitalistic decadence at home! Everyone's equal here! And everyone works, and therefore they have neither the time nor the need to do filthy things at night...!"

François grinned and Lammermoor whispered with a smile, "There is *too* night-life, Morand, believe me, there *is*."

"You haven't heard the end of this," whispered Morand. "Every man in bed now. Tomorrow's going to be a busy day."

Next morning the international delegations stood in two rows facing each other across an immense gray hall while the chiefs of the delegations and bemedalled Soviet party bigwigs strode down the corridor between them on a red carpet, shadowed by interpreters.

As in a military review, from time to time the Russians paused beside one of the groups and exchanged a word or two with the foot soldiers. As they came abreast of the French delegation, di Lammermoor took a step forward, his hands clasped behind him, his jaw jutted out, and his eyes narrowed to small slits. And taking a bow, he let fly a harsh torrent of words the interpreters were unable to follow, and while Morand, rigid with fear, clung to the coattails of his chief, Lammermoor finished up with a resounding, "Long live the Soviet Union! Long live the Revolution!" and raised his fist in the air.

With tilted head and open mouth, as if he were hard of hearing, the Russian listened to his interpreter, then took a stiff step forward, embraced di Lammermoor, and kissed him on both cheeks before he resumed his dignified progress. The black turned his head toward Morand and showed the whites of his eyes in a convincing imitation of ecstasy, and Morand shook his fist at him behind the backs of the others. And so that, too, had been gotten through, to everyone's relief.

The evening before their departure was reserved for a party for the international delegations intended to promote friendship among the nations. It took place in a small social hall decked out in conventional red bunting. A somnolent band was playing onstage. On account of the language barrier each national delegation kept to itself. The Russians sat aloof off to one side, and everyone had concluded the only thing to do was get drunk on the abundantly available vodka, when the music suddenly came to a stop, then played a fanfare.

All eyes turned to the stage. All at once, from behind the moth-eaten red curtain, there appeared a long, feminine leg clad in a net stocking; then, amid a crescendo of hoots and whistles from the suddenly reanimated Communists, it wiggled its foot.

The noise increased even more as an arm came into view, encased in a long glove of black velvet, its index finger curling enticingly, and the audience broke into a storm of laughter and applause when Luciano di Lammermoor, alias Mistinguett, complete with blonde wig, sprang out from behind the curtain and began to sing and dance: *"Je cherche un millionaire!"*

Everyone—Frenchmen, Germans, Italians, Englishmen, Spaniards, and Russians—

hung speechless on the lips of the black transvestite whose act walked a narrow line between brilliant and ridiculous, but even at the edge of the abyss maintained its dignity and provoked storms of applause from the entire hall, Gaspard Morand included. Now everyone had woken up. They pulled their chairs together, mingled, nudged each other in the ribs, shook their heads in laughter. The Englishmen whistled in mad ecstasy when Lammermoor imitated Louis Armstrong—"Jeepers, creepers"—while the Russians, their arms holding glasses of vodka frozen halfway to their mouths as they stared incredulously up at the stage, began to stomp in rhythm when he belted out an interpretation of "*Ochi chornye*," and the first glasses started shattering against the walls.

While Lammermoor took a short break, a second man came swaggering across the stage. Everyone recognized him immediately: it was Maurice Chevalier. His straw hat cocked over one eye, his shoulders thrown back, thumbs hooked into his suspenders, he bawled out "Prosper"—still somewhat uncertainly, for it was François's first appearance onstage—but with each *Yop-la-boum* he jerked his pelvis forward quite professionally, amid salvos of laughter from the audience.

He took a deep bow, and then Lammermoor as Fréhel (in the meantime he had changed into a little black dress—that explained the big suitcase, nodded Morand knowingly), squarely facing the audience with his legs spread wide, sang a rendition of "*Où est-il, mon moulin d'la place Blanche?*" that brought tears to their eyes, and the entire French delegation, Morand included, sang the refrain as if with one voice.

Di Lammermoor beamed and blew kisses. In fact, he had never before played to such a packed house, and to thank them all, as an encore (in his enthusiasm he had forgotten where he was) he intoned the "Marseillaise."

He tore the wig from his head and stepped to the edge of the stage with eyes ablaze, and his voice would have been enough to drive any company in the world into the bayonets of the aristocracy.

Naturally, it was the French who—automatically—were the first to rise. One delegation after another stood up, many quite unsteadily, laid hand on heart, and hearkened to the song being accompanied by the tinny band.

Morand thought he would have apoplexy when Golubchov leaned toward him with knitted brow and asked, "Isn't that the French *national* anthem?"

But then something straightened up inside him and he replied, "That, Monsieur, is the mother of all revolutionary songs. To its strains we stormed the Bastille, repulsed the Habsburg Monarchy, and beat the Germans!"

And he said it in such a tone of voice that Golubchov rose as well, and when the anthem was over went up to the stage, handed Lammermoor a glass of vodka, clinked his own against it and dashed it to shards on the floor before he linked arms with the black, whipped up the band to give it their all, and started dancing a *kasachok* with him.

Back in Paris, just as Gaspard Morand was counting out the banknotes for Lammermoor and starting to say something, there was a knock at the door and François entered. He embraced the black with a kiss on each cheek and lifted one hand in greeting to Morand. He asked for two minutes of the latter's time, hemmed and hawed for quite a while, then finally screwed up his courage and announced his resignation from the party. He had discovered his love for the stage, for cabaret, and wanted to try to make a go of it. He'd already quit his job at Citroën and nothing could stop him or make him change his mind and, difficult as the decision was, he wouldn't have any more time to devote to party activities and for the time being, no more money to give to it either. He asked Morand to forgive him and hoped he wouldn't despise him too much. Then he turned on his heel and left the room without a further word, hanging his head.

Morand silently watched him go, then looked at Lammermoor.

The latter lifted his hands in a fatalistic gesture.

"Lose one, win one. You can put me down as a member. But under my real name: Luciano di Lammermoor."

Morand stared at him. "And how have we deserved such an honor?" he choked out.

"You know, Comrade," answered Lammermoor with a smile, letting the word melt in his mouth, "I learned something from our trip too. Your struggle for a better life is worth supporting. And what I saw in Moscow of gray streets and gray faces, of misery and sadness, finally convinced me: I want to help to make this life a little more colorful and a little more gay. And this money here," and he handed the slender wad back to Morand, "can be my dowry."

"But...!" Morand sprang up. "But... But then he sat back down again, said nothing, and took a membership application out of his drawer. For by now he had learned that it was pointless to try to argue with the likes of Luciano di Lammermoor.

ERIS

265 Riverside Dr.
New York, NY 10025

ISBN 978-1-967751-42-6

eris.press